RED

Lemons are YELLOW

Apples are RED

Carrots are not

PURPLE

Carrots are ORANGE

Eggplants are PURPLE

Flamingos are not

GRAY

Flamingos are PINK

Elephants are GRAY

Reindeer are not

WHITE

Reindeer are BROWN

Snowmen are **WHITE**

Grass is not

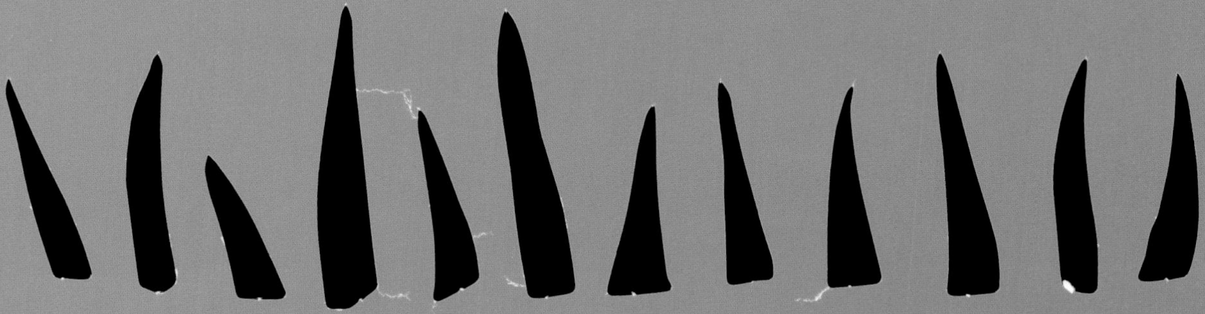

BLUE

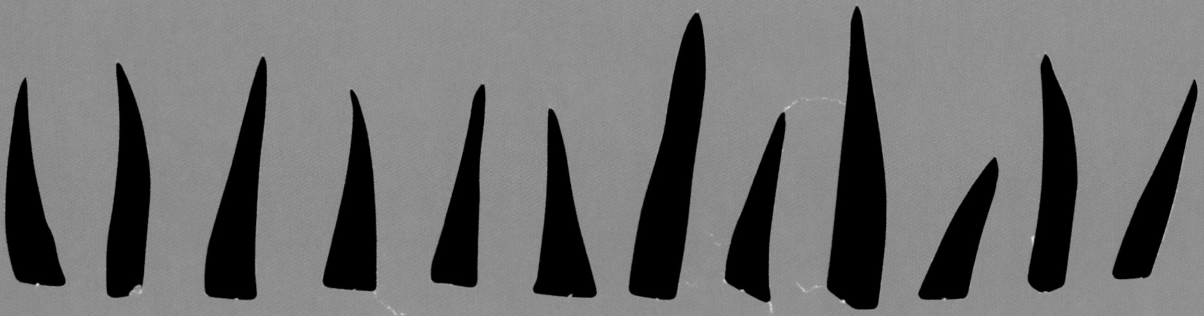

Grass is GREEN

The sky is BLUE

The moon is not

BLACK

The moon is SILVER

The night is BLACK

Good night!